SPIN THE BOTTLE

AN EROTIC ADVENTURE

VICTORIA RUSH

VOLUME 42

JADE'S EROTIC ADVENTURES - BOOK 42

COPYRIGHT

Spin the Bottle © 2021 Victoria Rush

Cover Design © 2021 PhotoMaras

For the uninhibited...

WANT TO AMP UP YOUR SEX LIFE?

Sign up for my newsletter to receive more free books and other steamy stuff. Discover a hundred different ways to wet your whistle!

Victoria Rush Erotica

1

———

When I saw a new email message with the subject *Fun and Games* from my friend Madison, I had to open it right away. She was famous for hosting the wildest sex parties, and it had been a long time since I'd participated in a group event, so I was eager to see what she was planning this time. As I began to read her message, I could already feel my heart pounding in my chest.

Dear Jade,

You are cordially invited to a party at my place this Saturday evening, starting at 9 p.m.

As with my previous events, there will be an exciting game designed to loosen everyone's inhibitions and get our juices flowing. I don't want to give too much away other than to say you'll definitely walk away with some interesting new techniques to add to your bedroom repertoire.

Get ready to mix it up with friends and foes alike, because in this game, there's no telling who or how you'll be paired up. All I can guarantee is that you'll be stimulated in ways you never dreamed imaginable!

Be there or be square,

Maddy

P.S.: Make sure you're all scrubbed clean, and I do mean everywhere, because we'll be exploring some erogenous zones you probably didn't even know existed!

By the time I finished reading her message, my panties were already soaked trying to imagine what kind of crazy new angle she'd dreamed up. After participating in her blindfold game and naked Twister, it was hard to imagine how she could ratchet the excitement up any further. But the idea of learning some exciting new sex techniques and discovering new erogenous zones had me intrigued. After stewing over what she had planned for the better part of an hour, I finally picked up the phone to give her a call.

"Hey beautiful!" she answered after seeing my caller ID on her phone display.

"*Fucking eh*, girl," I huffed. "You can't leave me hanging like that! What strange and wicked games have you cooked up this time?"

"Keeping it a secret is half the fun," Madison teased. "Besides, with your big mouth, if I told you, half the planet would know before anyone set foot on my doorstep."

"Hmmph!" I grunted. "I didn't hear you complaining about my big mouth the last time I was sucking your sweet pussy."

"Yeah well, you'll want to save that, because I have a feeling you'll be putting it to good use in some *other* ways pretty soon."

"At least tell me who's *going*," I said. "Will it be people I know or a bunch of strangers?"

"A bit of both," Maddy said. "You know how I like to mix it up every time. I plan to stretch your repertoire in more ways than one."

"You're such a dirty girl," I groaned. "Where do you dream up these wild ideas?"

"I guess I have a pretty fertile imagination. I'm always looking for new ways to keep my friends' sex lives fresh and exciting."

"Don't you mean your *own*?" I smiled. "I know you set up these sex parties for your own amusement as much as anyone else's."

"Maybe," Madison purred. "But if I can derive a little pleasure from everyone else's entertainment, can you begrudge me?"

"I suppose not," I said. "I'm just jealous you're the one always coming up with all these crazy scenarios. I feel like such a lightweight around you."

"No one's stopping you from creating your *own* party idea and inviting the next group over to your place."

"I might just do that," I said. "You're not the *only* one with a kinky imagination."

"That's good, because you're going to need every bit of it to participate in this new game."

"In what way exactly?" I probed, pressing for more details. "Give me at least a hint of what I can expect to get my creative juices flowing."

"All I can say is that everything will be completely random. Both in terms of who you'll engage with and in what way. Just be prepared for something entirely new and unexpected."

"You're *killing* me here!" I said, squirming in my chair as I felt my pussy throbbing in excitement.

"That's the idea," Maddy mewed. "By the time this game is over, I intend to have you tingling all over."

"Just *tingling*?"

"Oh, I'm pretty sure there's going to be a lot more than tingling going on."

"Well, there's a lot more than tingling going on right *now*," I panted while I rolled my fingers over my burning nub as I listened to Madison.

"Good," Maddy said. "But don't forget to save some for the party. I'd hate for you to lose your edge before we get started. Unlike my earlier events, this one's going to be *timed*. The more worked up you are coming into it, the more likely you'll be to walk away fully satisfied."

"*What?*" I said. "You're going to put us on the *clock* while we're having sex?"

"Don't worry, sweetheart," Madison purred. "Something tells me that with some of the new techniques likely to be unleashed, it won't take long to get your rocks off."

"You are such a *tease!*" I moaned, feeling my pleasure rapidly rising within me.

"That's the plan," Maddy said. "See you Saturday, sexy. Enjoy!"

After Madison hung up, I came hard within a matter of seconds imagining myself being stimulated by a group of strangers while everyone sat around watching. Part of the fun of her parties was the voyeur aspect, with those doing the watching enjoying the festivities almost as much as those being watched. The more I fantasized about it, the more excited I became, and it took every ounce of my willpower not to jill myself to orgasm ten more times before Saturday night rolled around.

2

––––––––––

When I arrived at Madison's house on the night of the party, she escorted me to her living room where a crowd of people sat around a large mattress covered with a rubber sheet and a single, triangular-shaped pillow. I recognized many of the faces in the crowd, but there were also quite a few new people I hadn't met before. There was an even sprinkling of men and women, and as the last few guests arrived at the house, we made small talk introducing ourselves. After everybody was seated, Madison sat cross-legged at one end of the mattress with a gameboard spinner and a large hourglass positioned between her legs.

"I'm glad everyone could make it this evening," she smiled. "I see many of you have already introduced your-selves, but just to make sure nobody's left out, why don't we go around the circle and have each of you tell us who you are and what your connection to the group is."

She peered at the sexy girl next door that I remembered from her last party and nodded.

"Hi," the woman said. "My name's Laura and I'm Madison's next-door neighbor."

"My very *hot* next-door neighbor," Madison added. "Who likes to skinny-dip in her pool late at night while driving the rest of us crazy with her perfect figure."

There was an awkward pause, then the hunky man sitting next to Laura peered over at Maddy.

"Um, I'm Laura's husband Brad," he said. "Who occasionally can be found guilty of joining my wife naked in the pool."

"And from what I can tell under the rippling water," Madison smirked. "Skinny-dipping isn't the *only* thing you two like to do nude in the pool late at night."

Brad smiled with a lopsided grin then turned to the man sitting next to him, trying to deflect the attention.

"My name's Lucas," the man said, making eye contact with some of the girls around the circle. His smoldering eyes and chiseled jaw had everyone drooling while they stared at him with their mouths agape. "Maddy and I work together, but she twisted my arm asking me to come to the party tonight."

"I didn't have to twist *too* hard as I recall," Madison smiled, peering at Lucas through hooded lids. "After I told you it would involve touching a bunch of *sexy women* in ways you never imagined."

Lucas chuckled, then turned to the pretty girl sitting beside him.

"My name's Amy, and I'm Lucas's girlfriend," she said, blushing slightly.

"Are you going to be okay if your boyfriend has to touch someone *else's* body tonight?" Madison asked.

"Possibly," the girl said. "I suppose it depends on which parts are touching whom."

"What if it ends up being another *man*?" Madison teased.

"*That* could make it a little more interesting," Amy said, grinning at Lucas.

As everybody continued introducing themselves around the circle, we all joked and prodded each other good-naturedly. In addition to Emma, Bonnie, and Lily from last summer's all-girl camping trip, there were two new women–a pretty twenty-something brunette named Amy and a hot African-Asian girl named Mia. On the boys' side, I recognized Ryan and Neil from Madison's previous blindfold game and Dylan from the Naked Twister night. Rounding out the group were two other guys, a young Robert Redford lookalike named Noah, and a barely-legal-looking stud named Alex, who said he was Madison's pizza delivery boy. The last person to introduce herself was Shae, the exotic transgender dancer I knew from the local cabaret club.

"Okay," Madison smiled after everyone finished introducing themselves. "As you can see, we have a pretty eclectic mix of people with different backgrounds and interests, which I think will make this evening's activities all the more interesting. I see many of you have been looking with interest at the vinyl-covered mattress lying in the middle of the floor and these strange objects sitting between my legs."

"Not to mention that weird triangle-shaped pillow on the bed," Lucas said.

"Yes," Madison smiled. "There's a *reason* why it's shaped that way. Allow me to explain the rules of the game."

She held up the game spinner card, pointing to various body part symbols scattered around the perimeter.

"As you can see, this spinner board shows various body parts displayed as erogenous zones."

I squinted at the card, recognizing an erect penis symbol, a woman's vulva, breast, and a few other familiar zones. But I shook my head when I noticed some unusual areas of the body highlighted.

"I didn't know that the *armpits* and the back of the *knee* were erogenous areas," I said.

"I suppose we're going to find out soon enough," Madison said, peering at me with a sly smile. "I'm going to spin the needle twice. The first person and body part that it points to will be the designated *receiver*, who will receive stimulation to the indicated body part. Then I'll spin it a second time, and the person it points to that time will be the *giver*, using only the new body part shown. Pretty simple, yes?"

"What's the hourglass for?" Laura asked.

"We've got a fairly large group, so in order to spread the loving around, we'll have to limit the duration of each round to ensure everybody has a turn before the night is over."

"And we'll be doing all this fully *clothed*?" Dylan said with a raised eyebrow.

"What would be the fun in *that*?" Madison said, lowering her head as she peered at Dylan with a Cheshire Cat grin.

"What's the purpose of the oddly-shaped *pillow*?" Brad enquired.

"As you'll see, a few of these body parts are in some hard-to-reach places. The pillow will offer some extra support to make it easier for your partner to caress you in the various nooks and crannies."

"Is the rubber sheet there for the reason?" Ryan asked.

"What reason were you imagining?" Madison teased.

"Well, if things get heated up enough, there could be some unexpected emissions..."

"There could indeed," Madison smirked, holding up a spray bottle of Lysol and a roll of paper towels. "But I've anticipated such a possibility, so we can clean up quickly in preparation for the following round."

"Exactly how long will each round last?" Bonnie asked.

"Ten minutes, give or take," Madison said, lifting up the hourglass and turning it over as the grains of sand began to spill from one side to the other.

"And you think that will be enough time for each of us to, um, mess up the sheets?" Emma said.

"Well, they say it only takes the average person two minutes to get off while having sex. I think we'll find this is a little more titillating that the average erotic encounter. Especially with everybody watching. Something tells me that ten minutes will be more than enough time to get everyone's juices flowing."

"What if..." Amy said, crossing her arms over her chest defensively. "We're not *comfortable* being touched in the designated area?"

"No worries," Madison said, taking a more solemn tone. "If at any time you feel uncomfortable participating, you can simply pass your turn or just say no if you think your partner is going too far. The whole point of this game is to have fun and open ourselves up to new experiences. You'll always be in control of who and what is done to you."

After Amy nodded to signal her consent, Madison peered around the group and smiled.

"So if everybody's ready to begin, shall we get *naked*?"

Everybody peered at one another for a moment, then a few people slowly began peeling off their clothes until everyone sat naked around the mattress, awkwardly trying to cover up their exposed body parts. But it was obvious from the hardening nipples of many of the women and the slowly expanding penises between the men's legs that they were already becoming excited about what was about to happen next.

3

———

Madison spun the game needle and when it finished turning, it pointed toward Lucas, pausing on the image of an erect cock. A few people hummed teasingly as they peered at the handsome hunk while his girlfriend simply glared at him. Then Madison spun the needle a second time and it landed on a picture of a foot, pointing toward Laura. The group ooohed aloud, taunting the two partners, then Maddy smiled as she peered at the selected couple.

"Alright then," she said. "Our first pairing will be between Laura and Lucas, with Lucas receiving stimulation to his penis from Laura's foot." She nodded toward the mattress in the middle of the circle and smiled. "Assume the position, you two."

The two partners crawled onto the mattress on their hands and knees toward one another, and when they came face-to-face, Lucas paused, peering at Laura inquisitively.

"How do you want to do this exactly?" he asked. "What position would you like me to be in?"

Laura glanced at the large triangle-shaped pillow and smiled.

"Why don't you sit up using the pillow to support your back and spread your legs while I sit in front of you?" she said. "That way, I'll have direct access to your cock and you can watch me while I stimulate you."

"Works for me," Lucas said, positioning the pillow behind him and leaning back with his arms spread out over the top edge.

Laura positioned herself between his legs then propped her arms on the floor behind her, slowly lifting her right foot to flap Lucas's pecker from side to side. He was already half-erect, and as she tapped her toes against his manhood, it slapped against the inside of his thighs while their other partners looked on with tight lips.

Lucas's cock was uncircumcised, but nicely proportioned, about eight inches in length and six inches in circumference. His phallus had a pleasing caramel color that matched his tanned skin, and as his penis began to expand and rise to its full length, many of the women around the group gasped.

"Mmm," Laura moaned, watching his cock slowly elevate as she teased it with her toes. "I haven't tried something like this in a long time."

"Neither have *I*," Lucas panted, clearly enjoying Laura's ministrations.

"That's a nice flagpole you have there, Lucas," Laura purred, admiring his package now standing fully erect and perfectly straight above his belly. "Let's see if we can unfurl the colors, in a matter of speaking."

She placed the soles of both feet on opposite sides of Lucas's erection, pulling them down toward his balls. The hood of his cock slid down over his purple crown, revealing his glistening bulb coated with precum. The women and a few of the men took a deep gulp when they saw his engorged glans, and a few of them shifted position on the floor, clearly becoming aroused watching the action.

"Do you like that?" Laura said. "Do you like it when I pull your foreskin over your dripping head with my feet?"

"Um-hmm," Lucas groaned, staring between Laura's legs at her parted labia while she angled her knees outward to gain a better grip on his dick.

"Are you looking at my pussy while I stroke your big cock with my feet?"

"Mmm," Lucas hummed, trying not to make his girl-friend any more jealous than she already was watching another woman stroke his dick while she looked on a short distance away.

I peered over at Laura's husband and noticed his dick was *also* standing straight up between his crossed legs while he looked on. Whether he was becoming excited imagining his wife doing the same thing to him, or he was simply getting turned on watching her with another man, I wasn't sure. But from the looks of the bouncing erections around the circle, it was obvious he wasn't the *only* one getting turned on watching the show.

"Are you wishing it was my *cunny* stroking your cock instead of my feet?" Laura teased, watching a dribble of precum falling over Lucas's crown and sliding down the side of his prick.

"Uhnn," Lucas grunted, not wanting to reveal what he was *really* thinking.

"Or perhaps you'd prefer my *mouth*?" Laura said, tilting her body forward while blowing gently on his throbbing organ.

"One body part at a time," Madison interjected. "Those are the rules."

"But I'm not *touching* him with my mouth!" Laura huffed. "I was just *blowing* on him."

"Yes, well," Maddy said, watching Lucas's cum beginning to spill down both sides of his pole like an overflowing volcano. "From the look of things, it appears to be having a similar effect. The point of this game is to see how far we can stimulate our partners using only *one* body part."

Laura reluctantly backed away from Lucas as his hard-on bounced against his belly.

"I thought the point was to excite each other using our *imagination*?" she frowned.

"I'm sure you can use your imagination to stimulate your partner in plenty of other ways just using your *feet*," Madison smiled. "As far as I can tell, Lucas seems to be enjoying what you're doing just fine."

"Is that true, Lucas?" Laura said, peering at his flushed face. "Do you like the feel of my feet on your burning pecker?"

"Yes," Lucas panted, no longer trying to conceal his mounting enjoyment of Laura's attention.

"Do you want to cum all over my feet?"

"Yes," he groaned, lifting his hips off the floor as he thrust his hard-on between Laura's soles.

I peered over at Amy and noticed her hand beginning to move between her legs while she stared at her boyfriend's glistening pole rocking between Laura's feet. At the same time, Brad rolled his fingers over the tip of his erection while he watched the couple, equally mesmerized. In fact, by now just about everyone around the circle was stimulating themselves in one way or another while they took in the show. I smiled as I glanced over at Madison, who was nodding quietly watching the couple. I had to give it to her. She definitely knew how to break down people's inhibitions and get everyone in on the action.

Even the spouses and partners of those having sex in full view of the rest of the group.

Maybe it was the fact that a bunch of strangers were watching them while they caressed and probed each other's bodies. Or the fact that they were being forced to have sex with someone other than their usual partners. Or maybe it was the novel way she'd set it up for each of the partners to stimulate one another.

Either way, I was getting just as turned on as the rest of the group, and as Lucas began to open his mouth in rising pleasure while he pistoned his prick between Laura's feet, I couldn't resist pressing three fingers into my hole while I imagined it was his beautiful dick plowing me instead.

"Yes, baby," Laura moaned watching Lucas's purple head popping in and out of his hood as his balls pulled closer to the base of his pole. "Cum for me. Let me feel you soak my feet with your sweet spunk. Fuck, this is hot."

"Uhnnn," Lucas groaned, lifting his hips further off the mattress as he pumped his dick faster and faster between Laura's clamped feet.

But just before he was about to pop off, Madison interrupted again.

"Time's up!" she announced, holding up the hourglass to show that all the sand had spilled over to the other side.

"*What the–*" Brad groaned as Laura turned to look at Madison with fireballs in her eyes.

"You've got to be *kidding* me!" she said. "You're stopping us *now*? Can't you see how close he is to cumming?"

"So it would appear," Madison said, glancing at Lucas's bouncing cock with streams of precum falling down over his purple balls. "But what fun is a game if we don't play by the rules?

"Besides," she said, peering around the circle noticing half the men gripping their erections in their fists and the women holding their hands between their legs. "There's nothing stopping him or his girlfriend from *finishing* the job once he returns to the group. There weren't any rules about that."

"You're *evil*!" Laura hissed, retracting her feet from Lucas's burning organ while she shook her head and frowned at him apologetically.

"That's why you *love* me, right?" Madison said, winking at Laura as the two partners returned to their positions in the circle.

When they sat down next to their partners, I noticed Amy reach over to grip Lucas's tool tightly in her hand, squeezing it so hard it turned his glans a bright purple. Whether she was doing so because she was pissed that he'd gotten so aroused from another woman's touch or because she was eager to finish him off, was unclear.

All I knew was that you could cut the sexual tension in the room with a knife.

4

Madison took a short timeout to spray down the sheet with some Lysol, then she wiped up the wet stain Lucas had made in front of the pillow.

"Okay," she said, peering around the group. "Just so we're clear moving forward, each pairing will have a maximum of ten minutes together, as shown by the hourglass." She pulled a chair up beside her and placed the hourglass on the seat. "From now on I'll leave it prominently displayed for everyone to see how much time remains. Are we ready for the next round?"

"*Hmmpf!*" Laura grunted, still glaring at Maddy with her arms crossed.

"I'll take that as a yes," Madison smiled.

She spun the game needle and this time the pointer stopped on the image of an anus, aiming toward Mia. Everyone gasped as they peered at the pretty biracial girl, realizing she was about to be touched in a forbidden area. Then Maddy spun the needle again, and it landed on a picture of lips, pointing toward Alex, the pizza delivery boy. The group chuckled when they saw his wide eyes looking at the board with a mixture of fright and excitement. As a bead of sweat began to form on his forehead, I noticed his cock twitching between his legs.

"This should be interesting," Madison smiled. "This time we'll have Alex using his mouth to stimulate Mia's rosebud. Are you two ready?"

Alex and Mia peered at one another from across the circle, then they crawled onto the mat, pausing when they reached the triangle-shaped pillow.

"I've never done something like this before," Alex said nervously to Mia.

"Neither have I," Mia said, unsure exactly how to proceed.

"Someone once told me there are two kinds of people," Madison said, interrupting to ease the tension. "Those who *love* to have their assholes licked and those who pretend *not* to."

When everybody laughed, Mia peered into Alex's frightened eyes and smiled.

"I guess it's worth a try," she said. "We can always stop if either one of us feels uncomfortable."

"You better get started then before your time runs out," Maddy said, turning the hourglass over and setting it on the chair.

"How do you want me to do this?" Alex said, peering at Mia like a deer caught in headlights.

She looked at the pillow resting beside them then positioned herself in front of it.

"It might be easier if I bent over a little to give you easier access. Why don't I rest against the pillow while you kneel behind me?"

"Ok," Alex said, staring at her sexy ass as his penis began to rise.

Mia slowly spread her legs apart then leaned over the front of the pillow, resting her elbows on the mattress on the opposite side. She had a magnificent, tight round ass, and when she bent over in a forty-five-degree angle to match the shape of the pillow, everybody on my side of the circle could see her entire perineum exposed from her glistening pussy to her tight brown pucker.

By now, Alex was fully hard, as his cock bounced excitedly in front of him while he gawked at Mia's exposed snatch. For a moment, I wondered if he'd even had sex with a woman at *all*, let alone used his tongue to stimulate one anywhere below her neck.

"Don't worry, she won't bite," Madison said, trying to egg him on. "I'm sure Mia washed herself thoroughly before coming to the party tonight. Give it a try, you might like it."

"Yes," Mia purred, turning her head to look back at Alex. "I scrubbed myself clean inside and out. Tell me if you can detect the scent of grapefruit and jasmine from the bodywash I used."

Alex leaned forward slightly, lowering his face closer to her dark crevasse as he wrinkled his nose, sniffing her ass.

"What do you think? Mia said. "Does it smell appetizing?"

"Mmm," Alex nodded as he stared at her dripping pussy mere inches away from his face.

"Why don't you start by kissing my cheeks," Amy purred. "Assuming Madison thinks that's not stretching the boundaries of our engagement."

"I think we'll give you a little extra latitude under the circumstances," Maddy smiled.

Alex paused for a moment then he lowered his face to Mia's ass, kissing her buttocks with soft pecks.

"Mmm," Mia groaned. "I like the feel of your breath on my ass. It feels sexy. Let me feel your tongue on my skin."

Alex extended his tongue, lapping one side of her ass like he was licking an ice cream cone, and Mia wiggled her hips to signal her approval.

"Yes, baby," she purred. "Lick my ass with your tongue. You're making me wet. Are you looking at my pussy while you stroke my butt?"

"Mmm-hmm," Alex nodded in a trance while he fixated on her exposed vulva as he swiped his tongue over her firm buttocks.

"Lick me at the top of my crack," Mia said, rolling her hips to encourage Alex to move closer to her butthole.

I smiled at her subtle way of coaching her reluctant partner to stretch the boundaries of his limited lovemaking experience. When he curled his tongue into the crease near the small of her back, I noticed a drop of precum fall from the tip of his cock onto the mattress. It was obvious that he was becoming increasingly excited touching the sexy African-Asian girl this closeup, and as he began to trace his tongue further down her cleft, Mia moaned in pleasure.

"Oh *God*, Alex," she panted. "That feels so good. Your tongue feels so warm and soft against my ass. Lick me lower–you're driving me crazy."

I shook my head as I watched the innocent adolescent explore Mia's body. Madison wasn't kidding when she suggested we might pick up a few new techniques from participating in this game. Not only was she introducing some unusual new procedures, but the feedback from the person receiving the stimulation was providing invaluable lessons for all of us.

As Alex lowered his tongue into her crease, Mia tilted her hips upward, encouraging him to go further.

"*Fuck*, that feels good," she groaned. "I've never been touched like this before. Suck my ass, Alex. You're making me tingle all over."

"Mmm," Alex hummed, beginning to lose himself in the feeling of burying his face in Mia's sexy ass.

As he continued inching lower, his tongue began probing the edge of her sphincter, and I saw it contracting excitedly in anticipation of Alex touching her private spot.

"Oh yes," she hissed. "Lick me right there. Let me feel your tongue on my rosebud. That feels incredible."

Alex paused for a moment, then began circling Mia's pucker with the tip of his tongue as he placed his hands on both sides of her cheeks.

"Uh-uh!" Madison chided from the opposite end of the mattress, and Alex quickly withdrew his hands, pressing his face harder into Mia's crack.

"Oh my God, Alex," Mia grunted, grinding her mound into the hard surface of the pillow. "That feels *insane*! Suck my ass with your tongue. You're going to make me come if you keep doing that."

"Mmm-hmm," Alex nodded excitedly, bobbing his head up and down as he slathered his tongue over her starfish.

"*Fuck, fuck, fuck*," Mia panted. "Yes, baby. Keep sucking me there. Stick your tongue in my hole. I'm so close."

Alex paused for a second then he extended his tongue and pressed it slowly into her hole.

"Holy shit!" Amy squealed. "Yes! Fuck my ass with your tongue. You're an incredible lover, Alex. I'm going to come all over your face soon!"

"Mmm," Alex nodded, his dick dripping strings of cum onto the rubber mattress below his tightening balls.

It was an incredible sight watching the two lovers with their asses turned up in the air while their juices dripped onto the mat, pooling in a puddle beneath their gyrating hips. As they began to moan more loudly and shake their hips in unison, I peered around the circle noticing everybody jerking and jilling themselves unashamedly as they watched the erotic performance unfolding before them.

I turned to look at the hourglass and noticed only a sliver of sand remaining in the upper half.

Come on, Alex, I wanted to scream to make sure he took Mia over the edge before time ran out again. *You can do it. Suck her ass like your life depends on it.*

Alex also seemed to sense the urgency and as Mia began flapping her hips harder against his face, he buried his tongue deeper in her hole, crunching his jaw up and down like he was eating her ass. This seemed to drive Amy even crazier, and within seconds, the room was filled with the sound of her screaming as her hips shook against his face.

As I watched her buttocks quivering from the convulsions she was feeling inside, I noticed Alex's cock bobbing up and down as he began shooting long strings of cum toward his belly in the direction of Mia's pulsating pussy. Suddenly, the entire room was filled with the sound of moans and groans as one person after another began climaxing watching the erotic show. Up to this point, I'd been so focused on watching the couple in front of me, I hadn't even thought about touching myself. But when I saw everyone else shaking and convulsing around the room, I thrust my hand into my pussy and came hard as I pressed my wrist against my burning clit.

Mia's orgasm seemed to last forever as she writhed against Alex's face, and when he finally pulled his dripping face away from her vulva, I saw her anus clamping open and shut like a jellyfish as her orgasm began to peter out. By the time they collapsed on top of one another, the only noise you could hear in the room was the sound of everyone panting in blissful satisfaction.

5

"**W**ell, I'd say things are starting to heat up *now*," Madison smiled when Alex and Mia returned to their positions in the circle. "That was crazy hot! Are you guys ready for some more fun and games?"

As everyone nodded excitedly, Maddy crawled onto the rubber mattress to wipe down the huge puddle next to the pillow.

"Anybody else need some paper towel?" she said, holding up the roll. "Cause from the looks of things, Alex and Mia weren't the *only* ones enjoying that last episode."

After everybody cleaned up, Madison positioned the game spinner in front of her on the mattress for everyone to see.

"I hope you guys saved a little for the next round. Because if that *last* one is any indication of what's to come, there's going to be a lot more juices flowing before this night is over."

She flicked the needle with her middle finger and when it stopped spinning, it landed on a picture of a woman's breast, pointing toward Emma. The group hummed approvingly, then she spun it again and it stopped on a picture of a vulva, aiming toward Amy.

"This should be interesting," she nodded. "This time it will be Amy using her *pussy* to stimulate Emma's *breasts*."

Madison peered over at Amy, remembering her earlier hesitation about touching certain body parts.

"Are you guys up for this?" Maddy asked.

"*Damn straight*," Amy said, clamoring excitedly onto the mat without even bothering to glance at her boyfriend.

I smiled at how far she'd come from her initial reluctance to participate, to her current eagerness to gain payback for Lucas's earlier rendezvous with Laura.

When the two girls reached the center of the mattress, Emma peered at the triangle-shaped cushion and shook her head.

"I'm not sure how much help the pillow will be this time," she said. "Unless you want to stand over me while I press my breasts up for you to fondle."

"Fuck *that*," Amy said. "It'll be easier if you lie down on your back while I kneel over you. That way you can relax while I move freely over your body."

"I like the sound of that," Emma said, lying down and peering up at Amy's dripping pussy as she straddled her waist and lowered her crotch down onto Emma's quivering stomach.

"Mmm," Emma moaned. "You feel so warm against my skin."

"Only *warm*?" Amy grinned.

"And *wet*," Emma smiled.

"Have you ever had another woman do this to you before?"

"Once before," Emma said, turning her head to glance at

me. "During an all-girls' camping trip. But we were more focused on rubbing certain *other* parts together than trying this."

"Well lie back and enjoy then," Amy panted as she slowly rocked her hips forward and back over Emma's tensing stomach muscles. "You've got some pretty tight abs there, girl."

"Do you like rubbing your pussy on my stomach?" Emma teased, glancing at Madison to make sure they weren't overstepping their bounds.

"She's moving in the right *direction*," Madison nodded, giving her assent for them to continue.

Amy pushed her hips a few inches higher on Emma's stomach, pausing when she reached the bottom of her ribcage.

"Uhnnn," she groaned, rubbing her twitching clit against the hard bone while she leaned forward, staring into Emma's eyes.

"Yes, baby," Emma purred. "Rub your clit on my chest. I can feel your nub rolling over my skin."

"This is almost as good as a man's *cock*," Amy smiled. "*Better*, actually. At least this way, I get some direct stimulation on my most sensitive area instead of him just ramming his tool inside me."

I peered over at Lucas who tilted his head while he peered at Amy with a sheepish grin. But that wasn't the *only* body part tilting, as his big dick began to rise between his legs while he watched his girlfriend fucking Emma.

Every man's dream, I smiled, shaking my head in dismay. *Watch closely, Lucas, and take some mental notes. You might learn a few things about how to satisfy your girlfriend watching her make love to another woman.*

While Amy rocked her hips against the bottom of

Emma's ribcage growing more aroused from the direct stimulation to her clit, she lowered her torso onto Emma's chest, rubbing her tits softly against Emma's breasts.

"Uh-uh," Madison interrupted, reminding the girls of the rules of engagement. "Pussy to breasts only. Surely you can think of some *other* ways to tease Emma's pretty tits other than with your breasts?"

"Don't mind if I *do*," Amy said, sitting up straight and dragging her hips forward on top of Emma's compressed cleavage. Then she placed her arms on the floor beside Emma's shoulders for support and began rocking her wet pussy all over Emma's glistening tits.

"*Fuck*, that's hot," Emma said, tilting her head up to stare at Amy's shaved pussy rolling over her shiny globes. "Fuck my tits with your pretty pussy, Amy. This feels incredible."

"Almost as good as rubbing *other* body parts with another woman?" Amy grinned.

"Yes," Emma panted. "In a different sort of way. I've never tried it this way before. I'm definitely going to be adding this to my repertoire, both ways."

"Oh?" Amy teased, spreading her legs further apart to press her pussy down harder onto Emma's breasts. "You like the idea of fucking a girl's *tits* with your pussy? Do you think you'd like it as much as when your boyfriend rubs his *dick* between your breasts?"

"*Better*," Emma smiled, glancing over at Lucas who was pumping his cock up and down in his fist. "This way there's some natural lubrication and I don't have to worry about getting squirted in the eye."

"We'll have to *see* about that," Amy grunted, shifting her hips a few inches to the side to position her vulva directly over Emma's right breast.

"Yes," Emma shuddered watching Amy's gaping slit roll

over her erect nipple as it disappeared in and out of her hole. "Fuck my breast with your pussy. I can see your bulging clit while you rub it over my nipple."

"That's not the *only* thing that's bulging," Amy smiled. "I'm going to rub myself against your teat while your breast caresses my ass."

Emma glanced once again in Madison's direction to make sure they weren't breaking the rules, but Maddy simply nodded as she began to roll her fingers over her glistening pussy.

I was happy to see Madison had gotten naked with the rest of the group when the game began, and as I watched her trill herself, I wondered when my turn would come around and who I'd be paired with. But for the moment, I was enjoying watching the two girls rub their bodies together, and as Amy began to moan more loudly, I pinched my own nipples imagining it was me she was tit-fucking instead of Emma.

"This feels amazing," Amy panted, rocking her hips harder against Emma's bouncing boob. "I'm going to come soon against your sweet breast."

"Yes, baby," Emma hissed. "Come all over my tits. I want to watch you coat me with your juices while you fuck me with your pretty cunt."

"Nnngn," Amy grunted, beginning to approach the peak of her pleasure.

I glanced quickly at the hourglass, estimating they only had a minute or so left before time ran out.

Fuck her hard, Amy, I said to myself. *Show your boyfriend it takes more than a big cock to get you off.*

By now, Lucas was pumping his organ just as rapidly as Amy was humping Emma's breast, and I wondered who would pop off first. But just as his mouth began to gape open on the brink of climax, Amy howled as her body began shaking over Emma's chest while Emma pumped her pussy in the air behind her. I glanced between Amy's legs, noticing her squirting all over her partner's chest and neck, then Lucas groaned as he began to shoot one long rope of cum after another out of his dick clasped tightly between his two hands.

Fuck me, I thought, feeling my own orgasm wash over me while I tribbed my clit watching the three of them grunting and shaking, coming harder than any of them had in a long time.

That ought to make up for your ruined orgasm, I smiled at Lucas, feeling some spittle dripping out of the side of my mouth watching his giant pecker oozing all over his hands.

When the girls finally recovered from their orgasms, they crawled back exhausted to their previous positions in the circle. I noticed Amy glance down at her boyfriend's spent penis then grin up at him, staring him straight in the eyes.

Two can play this game, I saw her mouth the words while he looked back at her with a lopsided grin.

6

———

After Madison cleaned up the mattress again, she sat cross-legged in front of the spinner board and smiled.

"Are you guys enjoying the festivities so far?"

"Mmm," many people in the group hummed to signal their approval.

"Is everyone looking forward to having their *own* turn?"

"Mmm-hmm!" they grunted in excitement.

"Does anyone *else* think ten minutes is too short a time for each round?"

Maddy looked around the circle, and everyone shook their heads.

"That's good, because we've still got a fair amount of ground to cover, both in terms of who's still left to play, and which body parts to use. Are you ready to move on to the next round?"

When everyone nodded their heads, Maddy flicked the spinner and it landed once again on a picture of an erect penis, pointing toward Neil. Then she spun it again, and it rested on the penis picture again, this time pointing toward Shae, the pretty transgender girl.

"Oooo!" the group huffed, teasing the two participants while I peered over at Neil to gauge his reaction. As a dyed-in-the-wool heterosexual, I wondered how he'd feel about being asked to rub cocks with someone else. But as he glanced at Shae, I noticed him running his eyes over her sexy figure, lingering on her hefty cock slowly drifting up the side of her thigh.

Unlike most transgender women, Shae was a true hermaphrodite, equipped with both male and female parts. Instead of balls resting below her sizeable pecker, she had a regular woman's vulva, including all the usual internal anatomy. Although she had a fully-functioning penis, in all other respects she looked like a normal woman, with firm large breasts, a narrow waist, and a curvy round ass to die for. It didn't take long for Neil's cock to begin rising in lock-step with hers as they peered at one another from opposite sides of the mattress.

"Are you two just going to *stare* at one another the whole time?" Madison said. "Or were you thinking of actually *touching* those pretty peckers together?"

Neil and Shae stood up and walked onto the mattress, and when they met in the middle, he paused a few inches away from Shae, unsure how to proceed. Shae peered at his cock pointing straight up toward hers and stepped forward, slapping her dick against his like she was having a sword fight. Neil took one look at her big dick and began to swing his hips back and forth as the sound of hard flesh slapping together echoed across the room.

Shae was uncircumcised, and after a few seconds of playful slapping, she pressed the tip of her cock against

Neil's, rubbing his dripping precum over her hanging skin. Then she peered at Madison, raising an eyebrow.

"Do you think I can use my *hand* for just a moment?" she asked. "If the objective is to touch our cocks together, I have an idea for how we might make this a little more interesting."

Madison peered at their dripping dicks, then looked around the circle, curling her lips into a smile.

"What do you think, gang?" she said. "Should we give these two a little extra latitude under the circumstances?"

"*Absolutely!*" Alex said, hypnotized by Shae's impressive girl-cock.

"Okay," Madison nodded, peering back at Shae. "But only for a couple of minutes. I want to see how creative you can be just using your penises. From the looks of it, you both seem to be enjoying it fine so far."

Shae pointed Neil's tip toward hers then she encircled the end of her erection with her hand, pulling her foreskin forward, overtop Neil's glans. Then she began rocking her hips forward while squeezing their joined crowns, creating a lubricated sleeve for them both to glide against. As he stared at Shae's tits, Neil groaned, thinking he'd died and gone to heaven.

Talk about stretching your sexual horizons, I thought. *I bet he never even dreamed of doing something like this before.*

As they rocked their hips together in rising pleasure, Shae cupped Neil's balls, squeezing them softly while she tightened her grip on the tip of his cock still buried in her foreskin.

"Fuck *me,*" Neil groaned, obviously enjoying the experience far more than he imagined.

"Okay," Madison suddenly interrupted. "I think that's enough use of the *hands* for a while. We've got to be fair to everybody else. Let's try to keep it just cock-to-cock the rest of the way, shall we?"

Shae paused for a moment, then she pulled their dicks apart, rubbing Neil's gushing precum all over the side of his shaft with her flapping tip.

"I have another idea for how we can rub our cocks together," she said, peering into his hooded eyes.

"Whatever you want," he panted, completely at her mercy. "You seem to have more experience in these matters."

"Mmm," Shae nodded, positioning Neil in front of the triangle-shaped pillow, then pressing gently down on his shoulder, encouraging him to sit against it.

After he squatted down onto the mattress and leaned back against the pillow, Shae pulled his legs apart and bent his knees upward. Then she squatted down in front of him, pointing her cock up in the air, inches away from his. As she shimmied her hips forward, their shafts touched. Neil groaned when he felt his balls press against Shae's wet vulva, then she began to rock her hips forward and back, sliding her dick softly against Neil's.

"Holy shit!" he grunted, hardly believing his luck being paired with the sexy transgender girl.

"Do you like rubbing your dick against another cock?" Shae teased, watching his precum pour out of his slit and down the sides of their joined phalluses.

"I like rubbing *your* dick, that's for sure," he panted.

"What about my lady parts? Do you like them *too*?"

"Fuck yes," Neil grunted, ogling her bouncing tits.

"Would you like to fuck my pussy while you stroke my cock and watch me come all over your hairy chest?"

"*God* yes."

"It's too bad Madison has all these rules," she said.

"Maybe we can get together later and touch a few *other* body parts together?"

"Absolutely," Neil panted, no longer worried about protecting his straight body image.

"I'd like that," Shae said, peering over at the hourglass. "But we better make the most of our limited time together. Madison's going to cut us off any moment now. Are you getting close?"

"I'm almost there," Neil grunted. "I just need a bit more friction..."

Shae wrapped her legs around Neil's hips, pulling their bodies closer together, then she leaned forward, pressing their cocks up against their bellies. As she rubbed her tits against his chest, their shiny dicks rolled over one another while they both began to pant more loudly. For a second, I thought Madison was going to tell them to separate since they were touching different body parts. But when she saw there was only a little bit of sand left in the hourglass, she hesitated.

As the two lovers grunted more loudly while they ground their hips together, I noticed quite a few other people around the circle jerking and jilling themselves as the watched the sexy couple. Apparently, Neil and Shae weren't the only *ones* turned on by the idea of a pretty transgender girl frotting her cock with a man. Having already experienced my *own* fling with Shae a few months earlier, I knew first-hand all the unique ways she could please her partner, and for a moment, I was a little envious of Neil having her for himself.

By now, the two lovers were locked in a passionate embrace as they wrapped their arms around one another, no longer concerned about Madison's restrictions. With one final thrust, they jerked their cocks hard against one another, grunting loudly as they began spurting over each other's chests. While I watched their bodies shaking and convulsing together, soft moans and sighs began emanating from around the room while other participants reached their own climax watching the erotic performance in the middle of the circle.

When the they finally separated, panting and exhausted, Neil and Shae peered into one another's eyes and smiled. In the space of ten short minutes, Neil had gone from being a dedicated straight man to a happy bisexual.

I wondered how *else* Madison was planning to stretch our sexual horizons this evening, watching her staring at my fingers deeply embedded in my throbbing cunt.

7

—————

"Whew!" Madison sighed when Neil and Shae returned to the circle. "Is it getting hot in here or what?"

"Yeah," Ryan said, fanning his face with a floppy wrist. "That was crazy hot."

I smiled seeing his dick still standing at attention between his legs, knowing that as a gay man, he must have been doubly turned on by the sight of a straight guy hooking up with a transgender girl.

"Give me a second to clean up the mess these two made," Maddy said. "Then we'll get back to the action. Does anyone need a bio-break or some extra refreshments? Help yourself to beer or wine in the kitchen."

We all took a short break and when everyone reassembled around the circle, Madison sat down excitedly, placing the spinner board between her legs.

"I don't know about *you* guys," she grinned. "But I'm dying to find out whose turn it will be next and what body parts they'll have to use. Are you ready for some more tribbing and frotting?"

"Damn *straight*," Ryan panted, his dick still flapping excitedly between his legs.

"Maybe we can find another straight boy for you to play with, Ryan," Madison smiled, peering around the circle.

She spun the needle and when it stopped turning, it landed on the picture of a pussy, pointing toward herself.

"Oooo!" the group squealed, excited to see Madison finally getting in on the action.

"Hmm," she said, shifting unsteadily. "I'm not sure I qualify to participate, being the *host* and all–"

"Fuck *that*," Neil said. "We didn't have any choice when you forced us to pair up with our partners using the parts you selected. It's *your* turn to be the submissive one this time!"

"Alright," she said, winking toward Shae. "But I didn't exactly see you complaining when it was your turn in the last round."

She spun the needle again, and after a long pause, it landed on another picture of a pussy, pointing toward me.

"Woo-hoo!" some of my friends welped when they saw that I'd be the one providing stimulation to Madison.

Maddy glanced over at me and grinned.

"I *told* you to there was no telling who or how you'd be paired up this evening. Are you up for this?"

"Are you *kidding* me?" I said, running my eyes over her naked body. "I've been up for this since we all took off their clothes at the start of the game. Assume the position!"

Madison crawled out onto the mattress then paused as I stood over her, staring at her upturned ass.

"What position did you want me to be in, exactly?" she said, looking up at me.

"Hmm," I hummed, stroking my chin. "So much pussy, so little time."

Then I peered at the triangle-shaped pillow and smiled.

"Why don't you bend over the pillow with your ass pointing up? That way, I'll have clearer access to your pretty peachka."

"Mmm," she purred. "And what position will *you* be in?"

"You'll just have to leave that to me," I smirked. "I've got a *hundred* different ideas running through my head."

Madison turned to face the pillow then she leaned her hips against the front of it, bending over with her elbows resting on the floor.

"*That's* what I'm talking about," I said, widening my eyes when I saw her dripping cunt flaring open for the whole room to see.

I squatted down a few inches and grabbed the sides of her ass, rubbing my mound against her crack.

"That doesn't exactly feel like you're caressing my *pussy*," she said, peering back at me.

"Stop being so anal for a moment while I work up to it. I'm trying to get you in the mood."

"You're the one fixating on my *anus* at this moment," she joked. "I'm *already* in the mood. Rub your pretty cunt against my pussy. We don't have all day."

"Hey!" Laura said, suddenly turning toward Maddy's vacant spot in the circle. "Speaking of time, Madison forgot to turn the hourglass over before they got started. Can one of you guys do it for her? She put each one of *us* on the clock. Now I want to see how far *she* can go in ten minutes."

As Lucas turned the hourglass over, I peered at Maddy's slit between her parted legs and got down on all fours, pressing my buttocks against hers. When I tilted my hips upward, our vulvas touched, and Maddy groaned.

"Yes, Jade," she grunted. "Trib me with your wet pussy. I've missed feeling your sweet cunny against mine."

"We haven't tried it this way before," I panted, feeling our labia and juices intermingling.

"I like it," she said. "I like the feeling of your ass rubbing against mine while you trib me with your pussy."

"Oh?" I teased. "You don't think we're overstepping the rules by touching our *asses* in addition to our pussies?"

"I don't see how we *couldn't* in this position," she chuckled. "Besides, you're definitely rubbing your pussy against mine, so I don't think we're breaking any rules so far, what do you say group?"

"I don't *know*," Laura kidded, peering around the circle at the other participants. "What do you think, gang? Should we let them touch their asses while they're rubbing their pussies together?"

"Maybe just for a *couple* of minutes," Shae smiled, winking at Madison.

"You better make this count then, girl," Madison said, peering around the pillow to look at me while I stared at our dripping slits mashing together.

"I plan on it," I grunted, pressing my cheeks harder against her ass while I tilted my hips, sliding my wet pussy over hers.

But as I watched the sand spilling from one side of the half-empty hourglass to the other, I shook my head wondering if we had enough friction on our clits to get off in time. After slapping our butts together for another minute or so, I pulled away and stood up.

"What the *hell*?" Madison said, turning to look up at me. "I was just getting into it..."

"I was too," I said. "But we don't have much time left, and I'm thinking of a different position that might be even more fun."

"I'm all ears," Madison smiled. "Or rather, all *pussy* at this particular moment."

"Turn the other way around," I said. "With your back against the pillow."

Madison pulled herself up then turned to lie against the pillow with her butt resting on the mattress.

"No–with your ass facing *upward*," I smiled.

"How do you mean," she said, looking at me with a puzzled expression. "How–"

"Lie down with your shoulders resting on the mattress and with your back against the front of the pillow. That way, we'll be able to rub our pussies together more easily, and I'll have more room to maneuver."

"Got it," Madison nodded as she flipped herself upside down, pointing her pussy up in the air.

I bent her knees and spread her legs apart, then I positioned myself between her legs, slowly lowering myself down into a scissor position.

"Fuck, yes," Madison panted. "That's much better."

"And we're no longer breaking the rules," I grunted, feeling her vulva touching mine.

As I began to rock my hips forward and back, the sound of our wet pussies slapping together echoed around the circle while the rest of the group started playing with themselves watching the two of us moaning on the mattress.

"Oh *God*, Jade," Maddy rasped. "That feels incredible. Fuck me with your hot pussy. I can feel your hard clit rubbing against mine."

"Yeah?" I said, pulling her knee up against my chest while I pressed my pussy harder against hers. "Do you *like* this new position?

"Yes," Madison panted. "I'm going to have to incorporate this pillow more often in my lovemaking repertoire."

"Me too," I hissed, feeling the pangs of another orgasm welling up inside me.

"Fuck me, baby," Madison panted. "I'm going to come soon. Grind your pussy against my cunt while I watch your pretty tits jiggling overtop of me."

"Unghh," I groaned, starting to fall over the tipping point. "I'm coming Maddy! I'm coming hard against your sweet pussy..."

As I held her upturned knee tight against my chest, my pussy began convulsing against hers, spraying my juices all over her stomach, tits, and face. She blinked up at me with a sputtering mouth, digging her fingertips into the side of my ass while she shook and moaned in simultaneous climax. Within seconds, the entire room was filled with the sound of everybody jerking and squirting while they came along with us taking in the sexy show.

As I shuddered overtop of Madison peering up at me, I smiled.

"How's that for getting our juices flowing?" I whispered, remembering her promise to me in her email invitation earlier in the week.

She could only smile back at me as my river of pleasure poured over her pretty face and tits.

---

*R*eady *for more erotic chills and thrills? Download the exciting first story in Victoria Rush's new erotic fantasy series, The Enchanted Forest:*

Sometimes it's not just the grass that's greener on the other side...

FOLLOW VICTORIA RUSH:

Want to keep informed of my latest erotic book releases? Sign up for my newsletter and receive a FREE bonus book:

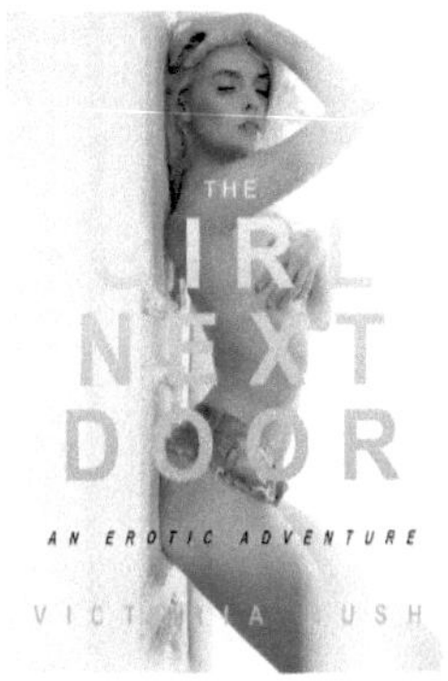

Spying on the neighbors just got a lot more interesting...